Mommy Has To Stay In Bed

Annette Rivlin-Gutman

Illustrated by Bonnie Lemaire and Shannon Stamey

To order additional copies, please contact us.
BookSurge, LLC
www.booksurge.com
1-866-308-6235
orders@booksurge.com

For Bruce, Anabelle, and Jory. I Love You.

My Mommy is in bed.
She can't get up and go.
It's not that she doesn't want to,
but the doctor says "no."

My Mommy doesn't feel well, so
I keep her busy in bed.
Together we make collages
or read books to each other instead.

We play cards, tell jokes,
watch a video or two.
We draw pretty pictures
of all the things we like to do.

We dream of far off places
and talk about when I'm grown.
We pretend to live like princesses
and imagine the bed is our throne.

Sometimes I get so angry,
I just want to shout,
"I don't like having Mom in bed
day in and day out."

Mommy tells me to scream,
hit a pillow, have a cry.
If I'm angry, she understands
and accepts the reasons why.

I'm different from the other kids.
Most mommies are not on bed rest.
My Mommy may not go to the playground
but still, I think she is the best.

I'm afraid to leave Mommy.
I don't want her to be alone.
She tells me it's okay to go.
If she needs me, she will phone.

We build a big fort,
where we can retreat.
I pull the covers over our head.
Mommy tickles both of my feet.

I make us a sandwich
her favorite, and we dine
on sundaes with chocolate sauce
to make us both feel fine.

We miss playdates on occasion:
the park, the sand, the sea.
But I'd rather spend time with Mom
no matter where we'll be.

We have so much fun,
my Mommy and me.
We cuddle and giggle
and act so silly.

:

I can't wait until Mommy's better,
but for now, this will have to do:
Mom in bed, with me by her side
watching sunsets together and enjoying the view.

Made in the USA
Las Vegas, NV
04 August 2023

75661828R00017